A BEAR
FOR
MIGUEL

An I Can Read Book®

A BEAR
FOR
MIGUEL

Story by Elaine Marie Alphin
Pictures by Joan Sandin

HarperTrophy ®
A Division of HarperCollins*Publishers*

For my father, Richard Bonilla,

who always met troubles

with love and laughter

—E.M.A.

For Brian, *mi amor, mi corazón*

—J.S.

HarperCollins®, 📖®, I Can Read®, and Harper Trophy® are
trademarks of HarperCollins Publishers Inc.

A Bear for Miguel
Text copyright © 1996 by Elaine Marie Alphin
Illustrations copyright © 1996 by Joan Sandin
Printed in the U.S.A. All rights reserved.

Library of Congress Cataloging-in-Publication Data
Alphin, Elaine Marie.
A bear for Miguel / Story by Elaine Marie Alphin ; pictures by Joan Sandin
      p.   cm. — (An I can read book)
    Summary: A young girl in El Salvador goes to the market with her father
and helps her family obtain necessities by trading a precious item of her own.
    ISBN 0-06-024521-2. — ISBN 0-06-024522-0 (lib. bdg.)
ISBN 0-06-444234-9 (pbk.)
    [1. El Salvador—Fiction.]   I. Sandin, Joan, ill.   II. Title.   III. Series.
PZ7.A4625Be   1995   94-36723
[E]—dc20   CIP
                                                                                          AC

❖
First Harper Trophy edition, 1997

CONTENTS

Chapter 1   Market Day   9

Chapter 2   The Guerrillas   21

Chapter 3   Hard Trading   29

Chapter 4   Milk and Butter 41

Chapter 5   The Ride Home 53

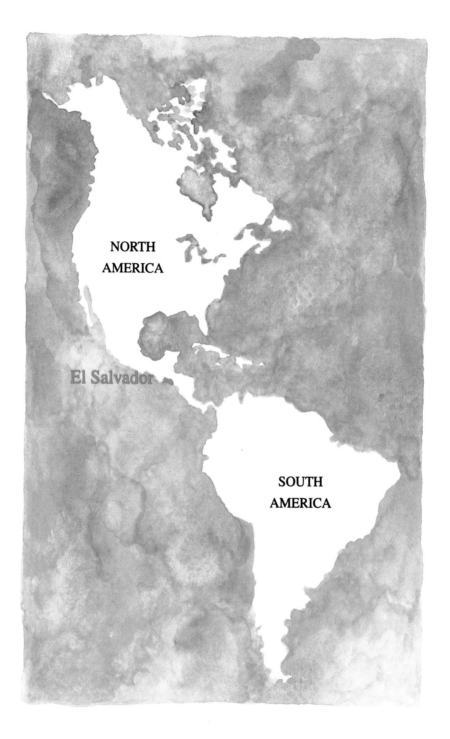

NORTH
AMERICA

El Salvador

SOUTH
AMERICA

Guerrillas are groups of independent soldiers who make surprise attacks against a government's army.

SPANISH WORDS IN THE STORY

¡Apurate!	*(ah-POO-rah-tay)*	Hurry up!
¡Espera!	*(ays-PEH-rah)*	Wait!
No se preocupe	*(noh-SAY pray-oh-COO-pay)*	Don't worry
Hermoso	*(air-MOH-soh)*	Pretty or handsome
¡Trato hecho!	*(TRA-toh AY-tcho)*	It's a deal!
¡Mira!	*(MEE-rah)*	Look!
¡Asi se hace!	*(AH-see say AH-say)*	Well done!
¿Que pasa?	*(kay PAH-sah)*	What's the matter?

It was market day in Felicidad,
a small village in El Salvador.
"¡*Apurate*, Paco! Hurry!"
María told her stuffed bear.
"We are going to the market
with Papa."

María ran out to the porch.

The wooden table and chair

were gone.

Only Papa's rocking chair

was still there.

"We won't ask
where Mama will sit now,"
María told Paco.
"There will still be
room for us
in Papa's lap."

"María, where are you?" Papa called.

"*Espera*, Papa," she cried. "Wait!
Don't leave without me!"

María climbed into their wagon.

She saw Papa's old tools.

How could Papa work without them?

"We can't leave yet," said Papa.

"Your mama is still talking."

Mama frowned.

"It isn't funny," she said.

"At the market you must try to trade
for milk for the children,
and some butter and eggs, too."

Mama picked up baby Tino and sighed.

"If only we had some chickens,"
she said.

"I know," said Papa, and laughed.

"A cow would be nice too,

and a horse,

instead of this old mule."

"Not everything is funny!"

Mama said.

"I only hope someone

will want to trade

for our things."

"*No se preocupe*, Mama," said María.

"Don't worry, someone will want
our pretty tablecloth."

"And someone will want the shawl
with the colored birds,
and our table and chair," said Papa.

"And Papa's old tools,"
María said.

"Of course someone will want
our things," Papa told Mama.

"And he will be a dairyman,
with lots of milk
and butter to trade."

"Remember the flour," Mama called.

"And try to get some sugar!"

"*No se preocupe*, Mama,"

María cried.

"We will get everything!"

19

CHAPTER 2   THE GUERRILLAS

Papa shook his head

as the wagon bumped

down the dirt road.

"We will try to get everything

your mama wants,

but it's hard to find

things to trade."

21

"But we need things from the market,"
María said.

"We need things," Papa said,
"but we must have something
to trade for them.

I can't buy things with money
because I can't find work.
If I work at the government factory,
the guerrillas will punish me.

But if I work for people
who help the guerrillas,
the government will arrest me.
So we must trade to get things
from the market."

"I wish I could help, Papa,"
María said softly.
Papa smiled and hugged her.
"Ah, but you do help!" he said.
"You and your little bear
make me laugh."

Papa drove past the guerrillas

into the market square in Felicidad.

"The guerrillas don't look mean,"
María said.

"They smiled at me as we drove by.
But Paco doesn't like their guns."

At the market, María said to Paco,

"What can we do to help our family?

It isn't enough to make Papa laugh."

She looked hopefully at the people.

29

A man looked at their tablecloth.

"*Hermoso,*" he said. "Pretty."

"For your wife's table?" Papa asked.

"I will trade a sack of flour for it,"

said the man.

Papa shook his head.

"And some sugar," said the man.

30

"*¡Trato hecho!*" said Papa.

"It's a deal!"

Papa gave him the tablecloth

and put the flour and sugar

in the wagon.

"Mama will be happy," María said.

"She worked late at night

to sew that."

"It's a start," said Papa.

The sun grew hot.

Finally another man walked up.

"That chair," he said.

"I will give you these beans
and some seed corn for it."

"¡Trato hecho!" said Papa.

Then a man talked to Papa.

"This man will trade two chickens

and a fine new frying pan

for my tools,"

Papa told María.

"He also knows a farmer.

I must go talk to him

about some work."

"What about the milk?" María asked.

"And the butter and eggs?"

Papa laughed and said,

"*No se preocupe*, María.

You make a good trade for me!"

María squeezed Paco's paw.

Then she shook her head

the way Papa had done.

"You are very small

to trade so hard!" the man said.

"I will also give you this flour."

María nodded. "That is fair.

¡Trato hecho! It's a deal!"

She clapped Paco's paws.

"We got more flour and the eggs!

Papa will be so proud!"

A young couple walked over
pulling a cart full of milk cans.

"What do you have today?"

the man asked politely.

"We have this table," said María.

"We need a table," said the man.

His wife nodded.

María knew she would get Tino's milk.

Then the woman's face lit up.

"*¡Mira!* Look!

For Miguel!"

María froze in the hot sun.

They were looking at Paco.

"Our son has begged us

for a stuffed bear," said the man.

"Would you trade that one to us?"

María wanted to say

that Paco was her friend,

and she could never

give him up.

"I tried to make a bear for Miguel,"

the woman said,

"but it was only cloth.

Miguel said it wasn't a real bear.

He was hurt by soldiers.

Now he can't run and play anymore.

All he wants is a toy bear.

We've looked for one,

but they cost so much

in the stores."

46

"He is our only son," the man said.
"If I could buy one from the store,
I would, but . . ."

María thought of baby Tino.

Would soldiers with guns

ever come to her house?

"What would you trade?" she asked.

"For the bear?" The woman's voice

was bright with hope.

"For the table and the bear,"
María said softly.

The man said, "Two pounds of butter,

four pounds of cheese, and the milk."

The woman looked shocked and said,

"We can't trade that much."

The man said, "For Miguel, we can."

"*Trato hecho,*" María said.

She shoved the bear

into the woman's arms.

"I call him Paco," María said.

"Miguel can give him another name."

"Thank you," said the woman.

María tried not to look at Paco

in the woman's arms.

Papa did a little dance
when he saw the milk and cheese
and butter and eggs.

"¡Asi se hace!" he cried.
"Well done!"
"I must take you to market
every time!"

53

Then Papa asked,

"Where is your little bear?

Have you lost him?"

María tried not to cry.

"*¿Que pasa*, María?"

"There is a little boy," María said.

"His mama said he needed a bear.

He can't run and play anymore."

"So that is how

you traded for so much,"

said Papa, and sighed.

"María, are you sure?" Papa asked.

"Do you want me to run

and get your bear back?"

María tried to smile,

but she could not.

"Miguel needs the bear,

and I'm too old for a toy," she said.

"I'm old enough to help the family."

Papa held her tightly and said,

"María, you are the heart

of our family."

On the ride back home,

María leaned against Papa.

She missed Paco's furry body.

She thought of Mama,

and how she frowned as she worked.

"Mama will smile," María said,

"when she sees the milk

and cheese and butter."

"I hope so," said Papa.

María thought how Papa tried

to make Mama and Tino laugh.

Papa wasn't smiling now.

She gave him an extra hug.

Then, in her heart,

María saw a little boy

reach for Paco.

She saw bright joy light up

the little boy's face.

And María smiled.

AUTHOR'S NOTE

In the 1980s, the people of El Salvador lived in the middle of a war. This war was fought between the government army and groups of rebel soldiers who wanted to change the government. These rebel soldiers, called guerrillas, believed that the government ignored the problems of the poor people, while the army defended the government.

Guerrilla warfare was an endless series of small ambushes and battles fought back and forth across farms, villages, and city streets. The guerrillas would hide out in the countryside and would come out to surprise and fight the army soldiers. People who were not soldiers were often caught in these attacks. Some people escaped from El Salvador, and many of them came to America.

In the 1990s, El Salvador finally formed a new government that included both guerrillas and army soldiers. People who had stayed, like María's family, saw the fighting stop as this new government began to address El Salvador's many problems.